W9-AMC-483

Every Year
On Your Birthday

WRITTEN BY ROSE LEWIS   ILLUSTRATED BY JANE DYER

Every Year
On Your Birthday

LITTLE, BROWN AND COMPANY
New York ᴕ Boston

Chinese calligraphy on page 32 by Ming Lewis.

Text copyright © 2007 by Rose Lewis
Illustrations copyright © 2007 by Jane Dyer

All rights reserved.

Little, Brown and Company

Hachette Book Group USA
1271 Avenue of the Americas, New York, NY 10020
Visit our Web site at www.lb-kids.com

First Edition: May 2007

ISBN-13 978-0-316-52552-9
ISBN-10 0-316-52552-7

10 9 8 7 6 5 4 3 2 1

TWP

Printed in Singapore

The illustrations for this book were done in watercolor on Arches 140 lb. hot press paper. The handlettering was done by Jane Dyer.
The text was set in Eva Antiqua Light, and the display type is Shelley Andante Script and Eva Antiqua Heavy.

For more information or to begin your own journey, visit www.fwcc.org.

To my parents, Joan and Jerry Lewis,
who showed me the joys of loving like crazy cakes.
All my love,
Rose

For Helene,
and her niece Jackie.
With love,
J.D.

Every year on your birthday, I think about the day you were born,
how the sun must have shone, or the moon looked so bright.

(picture sent from China)

I wasn't there, but I was thinking about you as I waited at home to be your new mother.

On your first birthday, family, friends, and even pets help you blow out your candle. It seems like the whole world is celebrating!

Every year on your birthday, I see you sleeping peacefully, snuggled with your favorite blanket and Sleepy Bear. And I still wonder what miracle brought us together.

On your second birthday, you become an American citizen.
Everyone watches you pose for pictures in your new dress,
and your smile makes everyone else smile.

Every year on your birthday, I think about the first time you waved good-bye to me when I dropped you off at day care. I couldn't wait for you to find my drawings of red hearts and kisses in your lunch box.

On your third birthday, we fly a kite at the beach.
You look at me with your dancing bright eyes and laugh
when your toes touch the sand.

Every year on your birthday, I think about how quickly your gurgles have turned to giggles. It seems like just yesterday when I met you.

On your fourth birthday, I surprise you with a puppy that wiggles when he walks. You kiss his tiny nose and squeal for joy as he licks you all over.

Every year on your birthday, I think about the six Chinese girls who shared a big room with you in China. They knew you before I did.

They are your first friends, like sisters, the ones who touched you and heard you cry and laugh for the first time.

On your fifth birthday, we picnic by the riverbank, watching the
dragon boat festival and cheering for the prettiest boat. . . .

We make plans to send secret wishes to the Moon Lady for the Autumn Moon celebration,

and look forward to sharing red envelopes during the Chinese New Year.

Every year on your birthday, we look up at the stars and remember your Chinese family. They are a part of our family now, and I hope somehow they feel the magic of your love too.

family

The Chinese character for "family"

is a synonym for

"home."